Whee-e-e,
What a Ride!

Happy Birthday,
Daisy!

Playtime
at Preschool!

Who Broke It?

"Look at the cookies!" said Baby Mickey.
"I just baked these for you," said the
baby-sitter. "You have time for one more
game. Then they'll be cool enough to eat."

The Disney Babies were playing hide-and-seek, and Baby Horace had just found everyone.   Now it was Mickey's turn to cover his eyes while the others hid.

"One . . . two . . . three . . ." Mickey counted.
Baby Daisy found a hiding place behind the
bookshelf. Horace found a hiding place, too.
Even Baby Pluto found a hiding place!

"Four . . . five . . ." counted Mickey.
"Yikes!" thought Baby Donald. "Where will I hide? Mickey will see me if I don't hurry!"

Donald started to hide under the table, but his hand touched something wet and cold. Oh, it was Pluto's nose! Pluto gave Donald a big lick.

"Here I come!" hollered Mickey as he moved closer to Horace. Horace covered his eyes and thought, "Maybe if I can't see Mickey, Mickey can't see me!"

"Found you, Horace!" called Mickey.

Mickey shouted, "I see a white tail!" Donald
thought, "Uh-oh! He found me!" But no,
Mickey had found Daisy.
    Donald whispered, "Pluto, move over!"

But Pluto wouldn't move. Instead, he wagged his tail happily and licked Donald again.

"Here I go," thought Donald, and he tried to squeeze in next to Pluto. Then CRASH! BOOM! What was that?

The baby-sitter ran to see what made the crashing sound. She asked, "Is everyone okay?" Then she saw the broken cookie jar pieces and bits of cookies on the floor.

"How did this happen?" she wanted to know.

"Look, there's Pluto!" said Daisy.
She pointed to the dog, who was
peeking out from under the table.
"Baby Pluto, did you knock over the jar?"
asked the baby-sitter.
Pluto looked at the mess and let out a sad
"Arf-ooo."

"Now, Pluto," said the baby-sitter, "we all
make mistakes and break things."

"I've broken something," offered Daisy.

"Me, too," said Mickey.

"Golly, gosh, sure!" said Horace.

"And I have, too!" continued the baby-sitter.
"But Pluto, there's no excuse for you to act like
you didn't do it, when you did. You'll have to sit
in the corner for a few minutes."

The baby-sitter quickly picked up the cookies and the broken cookie jar, so no one would get hurt. Suddenly Donald appeared.

"Donald!" said Mickey. "I didn't find you!"

"You had a good hiding place!" Daisy
guessed. She didn't know where Donald had
hidden, either. "Donald wins the game!"

Donald didn't feel like a winner at all,
because he knew who had really knocked
over the cookie jar.

"Cookie time!" called the baby-sitter,
passing out the fresh cookies. Now they were
cool enough to eat.

Pluto waited for his cookie,
but the baby-sitter said, "Sorry,
Pluto, no cookie for you."
Pluto looked at Donald holding
a yummy cookie. Poor Pluto!

Donald saw Pluto's sad eyes. He couldn't
even eat his cookie, he felt so bad.
"*I broke the jar!*" Donald blurted out. Now he
really wanted to hide!

"What? *You* did it, Donald?" asked the surprised baby-sitter. "Well, I'm very proud of you for telling me the truth." Pluto was wagging his tail so fast, he wiggled all over.

"Pluto, I'm so sorry," said the baby-sitter.
Donald hugged Pluto and said, "I'm sorry, too."
Then he gave his cookie to Pluto. Pluto ate it in
one big gulp!
The baby-sitter handed Donald the last cookie
and smiled, "Don't break the plate now, Donald."
Donald knew one thing for sure. If he did break
anything, he'd tell the truth about it!

Parenting Matters

Dear Parent,

Telling the truth about the mistakes they make is sometimes difficult for young children. It's only natural that when we adults become alarmed or upset about a situation, our children are reluctant to tell the truth because they don't know what to expect.

If we can control our alarm and put the emphasis on finding out what really happened, we make it easier for our children to be truthful. Take time to gently encourage your children to tell the truth in their own words and in their own way. Sometimes they also need help in deciding what is real and what is imaginary. Young children may actually begin to believe their own stories about what happened.

In *Who Broke It?* Baby Donald hides under the table and escapes blame for causing the cookie jar to break. Pluto, who can't explain what happened, is blamed for the accident instead. The longer Donald puts off telling the truth, the worse he feels. In the end, he blurts out the truth and discovers the relief and understanding that come with openness.

Who Broke It? helps young children learn that:

* even if they make a mistake, they are still lovable and capable.
* although telling the truth may be difficult, it will make them feel better.
* putting off telling the truth right away usually makes the situation worse.

Some Hints for Parents

* Let your child know that he or she is unconditionally loved and accepted by you. You may not approve of a specific action your child did, but you always love and approve of the person.
* Share with your child your own humanness and the mistakes you've made.
* When your child confesses to causing an accident, praise his or her honesty. Then let your child take some responsibility by assisting you with the clean-up. Talk in a kind way about how it can be prevented next time.